ni hao, kai-lan
Listen with Kai-lan

adapted by Sheila Sweeny Higginson
based on the screenplay written by Adam Peltzman
illustrated by Tom LaPadula

Simon Spotlight/Nickelodeon
New York London Toronto Sydney

Based on the TV series *Ni Hao, Kai-lan!*™ as seen on Nick Jr.®

SIMON SPOTLIGHT
An imprint of Simon & Schuster Children's Publishing Division
1230 Avenue of the Americas, New York, New York 10020
© 2010 Viacom International Inc. All rights reserved. NICKELODEON, *Ni Hao, Kai-lan!,* and all related titles, logos, and characters are trademarks of Viacom International Inc.
All rights reserved, including the right of reproduction in whole or in part in any form.
SIMON SPOTLIGHT and colophon are registered trademarks of Simon & Schuster, Inc.
For information about special discounts for bulk purchases, please contact Simon & Schuster Special Sales at 1-866-506-1949 or business@simonandschuster.com.
Manufactured in the United States of America
1009 LAK
First Edition 10 9 8 7 6 5 4 3 2 1
ISBN 978-1-4169-9076-5

Kai-lan woke up on the morning of the lantern festival and giggled with excitement. She knew that she would get to stay up late for the big celebration. All of her family and friends would carry lanterns in the dark moonlit night.

Kai-lan ran outside to help prepare for the festival. Just then a gust of wind blew Kai-lan's hair. "Whoa! Whoa!" Kai-lan yelled, giggling.

Kai-lan watched as a paper lantern floated on the wind. Then she noticed her grandpa, YeYe, chasing after the lantern.

Kai-lan reached up and grabbed the lantern.

"Here, YeYe!" she called. "I caught your lantern."

"Thank you, Kai-lan," YeYe answered. "I've got lots of lanterns for the lantern festival."

"Oh! I have an idea, YeYe," Kai-lan said. "We can put bells on the lanterns so they make a ringing sound."

YeYe smiled at Kai-lan. "Good idea! I'll help you put them on the lanterns."

Kai-lan and YeYe carefully attached a bell to each of the lanterns. Now the lanterns sounded as beautiful as they looked. *Ring, ring!*

Kai-lan heard a roaring sound. *"Rarrrr! Rarrr!"*

"Listen," said Kai-lan. *"Ting!* I know that sound. It's the sound of a tiger! It must be our friend Rintoo!"

Rintoo jumped into the basket of lanterns.

"It is Rintoo! Come on, Rintoo," Kai-lan said. "We have to get our lanterns ready! Let's go, go, go!"

"Yes! I love lanterns!" said Rintoo.

Kai-lan and Rintoo passed Tolee's boathouse. They waved to their koala friend.
"Come on down," Kai-lan called to Tolee. "We're going to paint lanterns for the lantern festival."
"Oooh, lanterns?" Tolee replied. "Wait for me!"

Kai-lan, Rintoo, and Tolee raced down the road. They jumped back in surprise when a monkey suddenly popped down from a tree.

"It's Hoho!" Kai-lan exclaimed.

"*Ni men hao!*" Hoho greeted his friends.

"We're going to paint lanterns for the lantern festival!" Kai-lan explained. "Okay, everyone, pick a lantern!"

Tolee, Rintoo, and Kai-lan each chose a lantern.

Hoho wasn't listening. He was too busy throwing leaves into the air. "Whee!" he shouted.

"Hoho!" Kai-lan called. "Which lantern do you want?"
But Hoho still wasn't listening.
Kai-lan spoke louder, "Hoho! It's time to pick a lantern."
"Huh? Oh!" said Hoho. He stopped playing with the leaves and chose a lantern.
Then he followed Kai-lan to the picnic table.

Kai-lan and her friends sat down to paint their lanterns. They each chose an animal to paint.

"I'm going to paint a dragon," roared Rintoo. "What are you painting, Hoho?"
But Hoho wasn't listening. He was busy chasing a leaf in the wind.

Tolee tapped Hoho on the shoulder. "Hoho," he said, "you're supposed to pick an animal for your lantern."

"Hurry up, Hoho!" Rintoo added. "We have to get these lanterns painted in time for the lantern festival!"

"Oh, okay!" Hoho said. He painted a picture of a monkey on his lantern. "It's me—on a lantern!" he said with a laugh.

YeYe stopped by to see Kai-lan and her friends. "It's very, very windy!" he warned. "Make sure your lanterns don't blow away!"

"Listen to YeYe," Kai-lan added. "He's right."

Rintoo, Kai-lan, and Tolee held tightly to their lanterns.

But Hoho wasn't listening. His lantern blew away on the wind. Hoho jumped up to grab the lantern, and soon he was floating in the wind too!

"Follow that lantern!" Kai-lan shouted as she chased after the lantern and her friend.

"Where is he?" Tolee asked. "I can't see him."

"Let's listen," Kai-lan answered. *"Ting!"*

Kai-lan heard Hoho calling and followed his voice. Then Rintoo leaped high into the air and grabbed onto Hoho's lantern. Rintoo, Hoho, and the lantern drifted back down to the ground slowly.

"Hoho, you need to listen, or your lantern might blow away again," YeYe reminded him.

"Okay," agreed Hoho.

"It's still windy," continued YeYe. "Watch your lanterns, everyone!"

"I have an idea," Kai-lan added. "If we put apples on top of our lanterns, then they won't blow away!"

"That's a very good idea, Kai-lan," said YeYe.

Tolee handed apples to Rintoo, Kai-lan, and Hoho.

"Okay, everyone, listen carefully! *Ting!*" said YeYe. "Put the apples on top of your lanterns."

Tolee, Rintoo, and Kai-lan all followed YeYe's directions. But Hoho wasn't listening. As he took a big bite of the apple, his lantern flew away again.

"Kai-lan, why didn't Hoho put an apple on his lantern?" Rintoo asked.
"Well, remember when YeYe told us to put apples on our lanterns?" Kai-lan
explained. "Hoho wasn't listening!"

Kai-lan, Rintoo, and Tolee wanted to help their friend. They knew that they needed to find someone who was really good at listening. They knew that the Peeking Mice could help their friend.

"Okay, please listen to me, everyone!" directed the conductor mouse.

"Let's use our ears to listen!" whispered a mouse who was playing a violin.

"And our eyes to see who is talking to us!" added another mouse musician.

All of the mice in the orchestra put their hands up to their ears and listened. They had their eyes wide open as they looked at the conductor.

"Now that you are all listening, please play one long note all together," the conductor mouse instructed the orchestra.

The Peeking Mice played one, long, beautiful note all together.

"Kai-lan!" Hoho exclaimed. "The Peeking Mice are really good at listening. That's what I should do!"

Kai-lan and Hoho began to sing together:

I put my hand to my ear that helps me to hear!
Ting!
I use my eyes to see who's talking to me!
Listen, listen, listen!
Ting!

"I like listening!" Hoho said.

"That's good," Kai-lan added. "Now let's listen for the sound of the bell so we can find your lantern."

"Ting!" Hoho shouted excitedly. "I'm ready to listen!"

Hoho used his ears to listen carefully. He heard a bell ringing in the distance. Hoho used his eyes to look closely. He saw his lantern near a tree.

"Good job!" said YeYe, as he patted Hoho on the back. "And you're just in time, oo. The lantern festival is about to begin."

Tolee was the fastest climber, so he scurried up the tree and brought the antern down to Hoho.

"Everyone, get your lanterns and meet me by the pond," said YeYe.

"Line up behind me with your lanterns," YeYe said to Kai-lan and her friends.
Hoho still wasn't listening. But when his friends reminded him, he thought about his *Ting!* song and quickly got in line.

"YeYe!" Hoho called. "I'm listening to you now!"

"Good," YeYe said. "Let the lantern festival begin!"

"Thank you for helping me," Hoho said as he gave Kai-lan a hug. "I love you!"

"I love you, too," Kai-lan replied. *"Ting!* Listen to all the lantern bells. This is the best lantern festival ever! My heart feels super happy today! *Zai jian!"*